D0409238

Finley Flowers

Original Recipe

BY JESSICA YOUNG

ILLUSTRATED BY JESSICA SECHERET

PICTURE WINDOW BOOKS

a capstone imprint

Finley Flowers is published by Picture Window Books

A Capstone Imprint

1710 Roe Crest Drive

North Mankato, MN 56003

www.capstonepub.com

Library of Congress Cataloging-in-Publication Data

Young, Jessica (Jessica E.), author.

  Original recipe / by Jessica Young ; illustrated by Jessica
Secheret.

        pages cm. -- (Finley Flowers)

  Summary: To win the school's cook-off and get a year
of free pizza, Finley Flowers and her best friend Henry
have to come up with a totally original recipe — the only
problem is that neither of them has any idea how to cook.

  ISBN 978-1-4795-5878-0 (paper over board) -- ISBN 978-
1-4795-8086-6 (reflowable epub)

1. Cooking--Juvenile fiction. 2. Contests--Juvenile
fiction. 3. Best friends--Juvenile fiction. 4. Elementary
schools--Juvenile fiction. [1. Cooking--Fiction. 2. Contests-
-Fiction. 3. Best friends--Fiction. 4. Friendship--Fiction. 5.
Schools--Fiction. 6. Humorous stories.] I. Secheret, Jessica,
illustrator. II. Title.

PZ7.Y8657Or 2015

 813.6--dc23

                        2014018946

Designer: K.Fraser

Vector Images: Shutterstock ©

Printed in China.
092014   008472RRDS15

For Wesley and Clara, who are always creating something great.

TABLE OF CONTENTS

Chapter 1
BIG NEWS

Finley Flowers's best friend Henry was turning nine in less than two weeks, and she had no idea what to give him. Finley was great at making things, but Henry already owned all of her best creations. He had duct tape flip-flops and a matching bow tie; candy mosaic picture frames; pull-tab chain-mail armor; a glow-in-the-dark dream catcher; a family of clay praying mantises (his favorite bugs); and good luck key chains and friendship bracelets in every color. It was going to be especially hard to top last year's present — a scale model of the Eiffel Tower made out of pipe cleaners.

Henry Lin had moved in down the street when Finley was five. He'd crashed his bike into her cardboard-box time machine, and they'd been pals ever since. Finley had other friends, like across-the-street-Kate and Lia-with-the-red-hair, but she and

Henry were best buddies. He was an excellent joke-teller and lunch-sharer, and he was always up for a great adventure.

In kindergarten, Finley and Henry had made mud pies and sailed pirate ships at the water-play table. In first grade, they'd started a dead-bug museum behind the cubbies and charged the other kids to see it. In second grade, Henry had taught Finley how to blow a bubble — then he'd helped cut the chewed-up wad of gum out of her hair.

Henry's birthday was Finley's chance to show how much she appreciated him. But she wasn't sure how. He never really talked about wanting anything — except for crazy stuff like a solar-powered ice cream truck and a trip to Egypt to see the pyramids. Finley had been worrying about Henry's present for weeks. Finally, as she was searching for lost homework at the bottom of her backpack, she dug up the perfect plan with only ten days to spare.

Glendale Elementary School First Annual COOK-OFF!

Put on your chef's hat and get creative, because it's time to show off your most original recipe! For this year's spring fundraiser, Glendale Elementary School will be hosting its first annual Cook-Off! Students of all ages are invited to participate — whoever sells the most samples will be awarded an especially delicious prize . . . a year's worth of Flying Pie Pizza!

Join us next Saturday in the gymnasium with your original recipe. Make sure to invite your family and friends to buy tickets and come taste all the unique creations. All money raised will go toward building a new Glendale Elementary playground!

* * *

When her teacher, Mr. Spark, announced it was recess time, Finley sprang out of her seat. She had news to share. Big news. If she didn't share it soon, she felt like she just might explode.

Finley got in line and filed out of the room with the rest of her class. At the end of the hallway, students spilled through the double doors and into the sunlight. Finley saw Henry heading for the playground and ran to catch up.

"Hey!" she said, leaping in front of him. "Did you read your *Glendale Gazette*?"

"Gah!" Henry yelped. "No. Why?"

"You'll never guess what the spring fundraiser is!"

Henry put on his baseball cap and his thinking-hard face. "Hmm. A fish fry?"

Finley shook her head. "Uh-uh."

"Selling those stinky candles?"

"Nope."

"A fun run?" Henry's eyes lit up.

"Ugh!" Finley said, making a face. "Those two words should never be used together. This is *way* funner."

Henry shrugged. "I give up. What is it?"

Just a chance to get you the absolute best birthday present ever, Finley thought. *But that part's a surprise.*

"It's a cook-off!" she shrieked. "To raise money for a new playground. They're going to set up a bunch of tables in the gym, and whoever sells the most samples of the most original recipe wins. And get this — the prize is a year's worth of free pizza at The Flying Pie!"

"Wow," said Henry. "The Flying Pie is my favorite. Too bad I don't know how to cook."

"That's just it," said Finley, hopping over a sidewalk crack. "You don't have to know how. It's supposed to be an *original* recipe — you just mix a bunch of ingredients together and cook up something new. Come on, let's try it! Let's make something Fin-tastic!"

Henry took a swig from his water bottle. "I guess we could give it a shot. Just don't get your hopes up."

"Yay!" Finley did a happy dance. "I can't wait to create something great!"

"You make it sound so easy."

Finley grinned. "How hard can it be?"

Chapter 2
FIN-SPIRATION

That Saturday, Finley invited Henry over to create the most outstandingly original recipe ever. She could almost taste the free double-olives-extra-cheese Flying Pie pizza already. Finley could make anything out of Popsicle sticks and glitter glue — cooking would be a piece of cake. And a first-place ribbon and pizza for a year would be the perfect present for Henry!

When Henry arrived, Finley's dad poked his head into the kitchen. "All right, you two," he said, "I'll be upstairs working. Just holler if you need anything, and don't make too much of a mess." He grabbed his briefcase and an apple and disappeared.

Finley and Henry sat at the kitchen table, pencils ready, waiting for an idea.

They sat for a long time.

Finley twirled a strand of hair around her finger.

Twirl.

Twirl.

Twirl.

She could hear the wind in the trees outside and the sound of Henry breathing beside her. In. Out. In. Out. No wonder she couldn't concentrate. It was enough to drive a person crazy.

Finley snuck a peek at Henry's notebook. As usual, it was full of lists: scientific names of bugs, favorite soccer teams, states he'd visited, and states he hadn't gone to yet.

Henry loved lists. He said they helped him keep track of things. Finley never understood *why* he needed to keep track of the world's most venomous creatures, types of sailing knots, or best Elvis songs, but he did. His newest list read:

Reasons I Love The Flying Pie:

1) Absolutely perfect crust (not too thick or too thin)

2) Tons of cheese

3) Mountains of toppings

4) Extra large is EXTRA LARGE

Finley rested her pencil on her paper and waited, hoping it would move on its own, like the time they'd played Ouija and the pointer magically spelled out Y-E-S when Henry asked if his soccer team would win the tournament. (They didn't.) But the pencil wouldn't cooperate. It just sat there in her hand like the dumb old hunk of wood that it was.

"Fiddlesticks," said Finley. "This *is* kind of hard."
Usually, she had ideas to spare. Her head was so full
of them, they were practically bursting out her ears.
Henry called that her "Flower Power."

So where were all those ideas when she really
needed them? Finley pictured them soaring and
swooping above her head, just out of reach. Or
scurrying like squirrels across the lawn. Or hiding
in the cracks between the floorboards. Ideas were
like wild animals. They only came around when *they*
wanted to — usually when she least expected it.

Finley and Henry tried doodling, eating chocolate
chips, and doing jumping jacks. But none of their
usual idea-catching tricks worked.

Finally, Finley flopped onto her chair and sighed.
"What next?"

"I don't know," said Henry. "You're the crazy-
creative one. I wish I could get inside your head."

Finley pictured what it must be like inside her head. With all those thoughts piled in every corner, it probably looked something like her room. "You're welcome anytime," she said. But watch your step — it's messy."

Then it hit her: maybe *that* was the problem. Maybe there were so many old ideas in her head that she'd run out of space for new ones. She tapped her pencil on the table. "Hey, why don't we try to meditate, like my mom does with her yoga? We could clear our minds so there's room for new thoughts."

Henry shrugged. "It's worth a try."

Finley put on some soothing, no-words music, and they sat on the floor and crossed their legs.

Finley closed her eyes and took a deep breath. Mom said that to meditate, you had to be quiet and not think. That was harder than it sounded. Finley tried to empty her mind, but as soon as she got rid of one thought, the next one barged right in.

"I don't know," said Henry after a couple of minutes. "My brain doesn't feel any cleaner. And my legs are falling asleep."

Finley opened one eye. "It's supposed to clear your mind, not clean your brain."

Just when Finley thought she might be getting somewhere, her seven-year-old sister, Evie, bounded into the kitchen with a sheet draped over her head.

"Hey, guys!" Evie yelled. "Wanna play with my dollhouse? I just redecorated. It's *haaaaunted*!" She waved her arms around like a ghost

Finley frowned. For a *little* sister, sometimes Evie could be a *big* pest. "Can't you see we're busy?"

Evie peeked out from under her sheet. "You don't look busy."

"Well, we are," Finley said. "If you must know, we're trying to focus."

"Sor-*ry*." Evie rolled her eyes. "When you get bored of *focusing*, you can come see my spooky dolls. *If* you're not too scared."

"What's a ghost's favorite fruit?" Henry asked.

"Boo-berries!" Evie screeched.

Finley groaned. She liked Henry's jokes, but this was no time for distractions. A year of free Flying Pie pizza was on the line. "Evie, we're working. *Go. Find. Dad.*"

Evie flounced out of the room, her sheet trailing behind her.

Finley glared at her last chocolate chip, popped it into her mouth, and closed her eyes. As it melted, she pictured the chocolate going right to her brain and working its magic, turning every single thinking switch to ON.

Suddenly, she got a warm, tingly feeling all over her body.

Yes, she'd caught one! A shiny new idea!

"Okay," Finley said, turning to Henry, "the other contestants will probably make the usual stuff — chocolate chip cookies, chili, potato salad. Those are safe bets. Everyone likes them."

"Sweet!" said Henry. "Let's make chocolate chip cookies. Even *I* like chocolate chip cookies."

Finley shook her head. "Nope. They want an original recipe, so we need to make something different. Something Fin-credible."

"Hmm." Henry crinkled his forehead. "How do we do that?"

"Mr. Spark says that cooking is a science. So we should do what all great scientists do — experiment." Finley opened the fridge door. "First we'll need to do some research. Let's see . . ."

She scanned the shelves for something exciting. But it was the same old stuff. Boring, boring, boring.

She'd heard you could tell a lot about a person from
the inside of their fridge. She was going to have to
talk to Mom and Dad about that.

"How do you know if there's an elephant in your
refrigerator?" said Henry, peering over her shoulder.

Finley had heard that one before. "You can't shut
the door," she said.

"Nope," said Henry. "Footprints in the butter."

"Good one." Finley grinned. She rummaged around and set a bunch of supplies on the counter: chocolate sauce, mustard, strawberries, yogurt, and sparkling water.

"What are you looking for, exactly?" Henry asked.

Finley held up a jar of green olives. "Fin-spiration."

Chapter 3
TASTE TEST

Finley and Henry arranged all the foods in a long
row on the kitchen table.

"All right," said Finley. "The lab is ready.
Remember when we studied the scientific method in
class?"

Henry nodded. "First we need to make a
hypothesis about what's going to happen." He
took out his notebook and started listing all the
ingredients.

"Look at all this good stuff," said Finley, getting out some mixing bowls. "I predict we'll stir up something yummy."

"Hypothesis . . . yummy . . ." Henry muttered as he wrote.

Finley and Henry got to work.

They mixed and mashed.

They beat and blended.

They spread and sprinkled.

Henry recorded all their observations in his notebook.

They made strawberry-garlic burritos, salad dressing soup, tuna ice cream, and marshmallow-gummy bear kebabs covered with barbeque sauce. Then they appointed Evie to be the official taste-tester.

"Bleccch!" said Evie, after sampling the soup. "What are you two trying to do, kill me? If this is a taste test, you totally flunked!" She grabbed a granola bar from the cupboard and clomped upstairs.

"Results . . ." Henry scribbled in his notebook. "The . . . data . . . was . . . yuck."

"Forget about her," Finley told him. "She puts ketchup on everything. Her taste buds are probably broken."

"Maybe we're making things too complicated," said Henry. "Sometimes the simplest answer is the best. Kate and Lia told me the other day they're going to bake brownies. They said Olivia's entering, too. I wonder what she's going to bring."

"Who cares?" said Finley, dumping Evie's leftover soup into the sink. Olivia Snotham was so annoying. She always won everything, and she was so braggy about it.

"We could look at some recipes," Henry suggested. "Recipes have lists."

"We don't need to copy," said Finley. "We've got our own ideas."

"Not always *good* ones," said Henry. "Remember your origami coffee mugs? That idea leaked."

Finley frowned. "They don't *all* have to be good ideas. We just need one."

Finley and Henry spent the rest of the afternoon experimenting. They whipped up pepperoni parfaits,

chocolate-dipped olives, and pickle juice punch. But they couldn't seem to come up with something original *and* tasty.

Instead they made a mess.

"Crikey," Henry said as they surveyed the damage.

Just then Finley's older brother, Zack, burst through the door.

"Whoa!" he said, stopping in his tracks. "It looks like a tornado hit the kitchen. Mom will be home any minute, and she's not going to be happy."

Finley scowled at Zack. Ever since he'd started middle school, he acted like he knew everything about everything.

"She'll be happy if we win the cook-off and get a year's worth of free pizza," Finley told him. "Besides, I asked Dad, and he told us we could work on our recipe."

"Good luck," Zack replied. He grabbed a handful of chocolate chips and headed upstairs. "Looks like you're gonna need it."

Finley glanced around the room. The kitchen counter was littered with bags, wrappers, and boxes, and the table was covered with spatters and spills. "He's right," she said to Henry. "This is a Fin-tastic disaster."

Finley and Henry got to work. They wiped and washed and dried and swept until the kitchen looked almost back-to-normal.

Then Henry glanced at his watch. "Dinnertime," he said. "I gotta go home. Too bad our food experiments failed. I guess yumminess is hard to predict."

Finley handed him his bag. "Don't worry," she said. "We've still got eight whole days till the cook-off. We'll think of something."

But deep down Finley wasn't so sure. Even though they'd started with terrific ingredients, everything they'd made had tasted terrible.

Cooking was turning out to be a lot harder than it looked.

Chapter 4
SECRET RECIPE

That night at dinner, Finley paid extra attention to the food on her plate. How did Mom and Dad do it? Everything they made was so . . . *good.*

"Pass me zee carrots please, Papa," she said. "Merci."

"What's up with the French accent?" Zack asked, helping himself to a heap of mashed potatoes. "Planning a trip?"

Finley shrugged. "Maybe."

"Finley's going to move to *Par-ee* and become a famous French chef," Evie said. "But she needs a little practice first." She dabbed at the corners of her mouth with her napkin.

"Paris," said Mom. "Ooh-la-la."

"A chef?" said Dad. "I thought you were going to be a professional pet rock painter. That's what you said when you made that pet rock zoo for Gran."

Finley poured some dressing on her salad. "I was five, Dad. I changed my mind."

"So what's on the menu for the cooking contest?" asked Mom. "Dad told me you and Henry have been busy."

"I can't tell you," said Finley. "It's confidential."

"A matter of national security," Zack said, shoveling potatoes into his mouth. "Why don't they just have you sell those stinky candles to raise money? That's what we always did."

"You could give us a little hint," said Dad. "We won't tell anyone."

"Nope." Finley shook her head. "You'll just have to wait. Besides, when we win, everyone will know. We'll be Glendale Elementary School Cook-Off legends!"

Zack snorted. "Sorry," he said, laughing. "Too much pepper."

Finley glared at him across the table. He was always making fun of her, but she'd show him. Soon she'd be eating her Flying Pie pizza. And he'd be eating his words.

* * *

Monday morning, Finley was extra hoppity in class. She tried to focus on her work, but her head was full of ideas and ingredients. Her leg wouldn't stop jiggling as she did her silent reading. And by the time math was half over, she'd twirled her hair into a nest of tangles.

Maybe there was something she'd eaten recently she could use as a starting point. Finley strained her brain trying to remember everything she'd had in the past day: carrots, peas, mashed potatoes, grapes, chicken, salad. She'd had oatmeal for breakfast. But what went great with oatmeal?

"Finley?" Mr. Spark gave her his trying-to-be-patient look. He was standing by the board with a marker in his hand. He seemed like he was waiting for an answer.

Finley sat up straight and said the first thing that came to mind: "Maple syrup!"

Giggles erupted across the room.

Mr. Spark rubbed his eyes like he needed a nap. "Finley, we are on question ten, on probability. Do you have an answer for us, in the form of a *number*?"

"Um . . ." Finley looked to Henry for some type of clue, but he just made his wish-I-could-help-you-but-you're-on-your-own face. In the row next to her, Olivia Snotham smirked and covered up her worksheet.

Finley flipped through her textbook. There were so many numbers to choose from. What were the chances she'd guess right? The probability of *that* was next to nothing. She remembered Henry saying that sometimes the simplest answer was the best. "One?" Finley said softly, crossing her fingers under her desk.

Mr. Spark raised his eyebrows. "Nice guess," he said. "But not quite. Olivia?"

"Eight," said Olivia, narrowing her eyes at Finley in her know-it-all way.

"Thank you, Olivia," said Mr. Spark. "Now let's all follow along together. We're on page nineteen, question eleven."

* * *

When math was finally over, Finley had never been so happy to go to the cafeteria. She'd made her own lunch — a sandwich, grapes, carrot sticks, and pumpkin bread. Mom even let her bring chocolate milk.

Henry unpacked his usual cheese, crackers, apple, yogurt, and granola bar.

"I thought I'd try a lunch experiment," said Finley. "Behold the Sandwich of the Day: a BNT — bacon, Nutella, and tomato."

"Wow," said Henry.

As Finley unfolded the fancy, rose-covered napkin left over from one of Mom's book club dinners, Olivia Snotham squeezed in between her and Henry. Olivia usually didn't sit with them. She usually didn't even talk to them, except to make fun of them. Or if she wanted something.

"Nice napkin, Finley *Flowers*," said Olivia. "It matches your name."

At least it doesn't match your name, Finley thought. But she kept her mouth shut. Olivia always had to have the last word, and it wasn't worth fighting her for it.

"What is *that*?" Olivia pointed to Finley's sandwich.

"Oh, just something I whipped up," said Finley. She didn't want to give Olivia any ideas for the big cook-off.

Olivia scrunched up her nose. "Interesting," she said, in a voice that Finley knew meant "ew." Olivia always found the nicest ways of saying and doing not-so-nice things. She'd been like that since kindergarten, when she kept trying to "help" Finley by wiping off her freckles and straightening her hair.

Olivia took out her perfectly packed lunch and arranged it on the table. "Kate said you two are entering the cook-off," she said. "What are you going to make?"

"Our recipe is top secret," said Henry.

Finley nodded. *Right*, she thought. *It's so secret, even* we *don't know what it is.*

"Well, *I'm* making something amazing." Olivia shook her perfect corkscrew curls. They bobbed up and down from her hair bow like a bunch of blonde Slinkies. "I think I have a *very* good chance of winning."

Finley tried not to roll her eyes. *Braggy, brag, brag,* she thought. *What a show-off.*

"Good luck," said Henry.

Olivia smiled. "I don't need luck," she said in her phony polite voice. "I have talent." She unwrapped her sandwich and took a dainty, birdlike bite.

Finley ripped off a hunk of her own sandwich. It didn't taste nearly as good as she'd hoped it would. Olivia had ruined Finley's perfectly good lunch.

It made Finley want to take what was left of her chocolate milk and accidentally dump it on Olivia's head.

But more than anything, it made her want to win.

Chapter 5
SPIN TO WIN

Finley packed a new sandwich every day that week: Pesto Pineapple, Egg Salad with Honey, Tuna Banana, and Unidentified-Leftovers Surprise. But none of them turned out so well.

She and Henry clearly needed more practice, especially with the cook-off less than a week away, but between Henry's soccer and homework, there was no time to be creative in the kitchen.

When Finley got home on Friday, Mom was working late, Evie was at a friend's, and Zack was at baseball. Dad said Henry could come over after soccer to work on their recipe.

Henry showed up at Finley's wearing a white apron and chef's hat. "Turn on your Flower Power," he said. "Let's create something great!"

"Wow," said Finley, looking him up and down. "What's with the outfit?"

"My mom found it. I've been waiting all week to try it out," he said, rubbing his hands together.

"I'm dressed for success! Get ready for a flavor explosion!" He saluted Finley and marched to the kitchen.

Finley followed. "Hey, are you feeling okay? Why are you talking like that?

"Like what?" Henry asked.

"Like, 'flavor explosion!' and 'dressed for success!' It's like you're some kind of cooking superhero," she said.

"Da-da-daaaaaah!" Henry grabbed a whisk and raised it above his head like a sword. "This is a job for Captain Cook!"

Finley laughed.

Henry put the whisk down and smoothed his apron. "I'm just getting to know my inner chef," he told her.

Finley raised her eyebrows. "Your inner chef?" she said.

"Yeah." Henry nodded. "The one that's been hiding inside me, waiting to come out. I've been watching some cooking shows, and —"

Finley crossed her arms. "Cooking shows?"

"I wanted to see how real chefs do it."

"*Real* chefs?" she echoed. "We *are* real chefs."

"*Professional* chefs," said Henry. "What's wrong with getting a little extra inspiration, not to mention information? The cook-off is in *two days*. We've got to think fast." He held out his notebook. "I took notes."

Finley leafed through the pages, then handed it back. Sometimes there were things Henry just didn't understand. "Listen, we don't need to follow what other people do, even if they're on TV. Ingredients are our inspiration."

"Those shows don't just tell you what to make," said Henry. "They teach you techniques and stuff. It might help us figure out a plan."

"We already *have* a plan," said Finley. "Keep trying different things until we get something great."

"Okay," said Henry, adjusting his chef's hat. "I'm ready. Get out the pots and pans."

"That won't be necessary," Finley said. "Dad said we're not allowed to use the stove."

"What?" Henry frowned. "But that means no sautéing, no flambéing, no soufflé-ing, no boiling, broiling, frying, stewing, steaming, baking, poaching, roasting . . . how are we supposed to cook?"

"Simmer down," Finley said. "Food doesn't have to be hot to be good. There's still mixing, mashing, stirring, spreading, and chilling. Now, let's think for a minute . . ." She glanced at the clock. "We've got an hour till Mom gets home from work. It's Friday, so she'll be extra tired and cranky."

Finley opened the cupboards wide and looked inside. "Hey, I know! Maybe we can make dinner. That way Mom and Dad won't have to cook."

"Sounds good," said Henry. "What can we make?"

"Mom likes to eat healthy stuff. Remember when Mr. Spark talked about nutrition? What were all those food groups?"

"Fruits, veggies, grains . . ." said Henry.

"Right. We could combine them into some type of well-balanced meal. Come on, let's go tell Dad."

Finley bounded into her parents' home office, and Henry followed. Dad was staring at his computer screen with his thinking-hard face.

"Dad," Finley said, "don't worry about dinner. Henry and I have got it covered."

"Great, honey," Dad mumbled as he typed. "Don't forget to wear your helmets."

Finley shook her head. "Sometimes he doesn't listen so well," she whispered, leading Henry back to the kitchen.

Henry got out his notebook. "So we've got fruits, veggies, grains . . ."

"What's the cheese one?" Finley asked. "Dairy?"

"Right." Henry nodded. "And that one with meat and beans?"

"Proteins," said Finley.

Just then Evie came skipping into the kitchen. "Groovy apron, Henry. Anybody want to play a board game?"

"No, thanks," said Finley. "We're busy making dinner. Besides, board games are *bor*ing."

"No, they're not," said Evie. "Board games are fun. The ones with spinners are my favorite. Spin, spin, spin . . ." She spun around. "You never know what you're going to get."

"You're going to get dizzy," said Finley. "Hey, wait! What if we turn dinner into a cooking game? We could write the names of our favorite foods from each food group on the spinner, then spin the wheel to pick ingredients. We'll come up with a well-balanced meal no one has ever thought of. Evie, you're a genius!"

Evie beamed. "Finally, someone noticed."

Chapter 6
DINNER IN A GLASS

"Okay," Finley said, passing out sticky labels. "Let's pick our favorite foods, write them down on these, and stick them on the spinner. We'll take turns until all of the spaces are filled. Then we'll spin to decide which foods to use. If we start with all the best ingredients, we can't help but wind up with a winning recipe."

"Makes sense." Evie grabbed the spinner. "I'm the youngest, so I get to go first."

Finley rolled her eyes. "Fine."

Evie wrote *ketchup* on a label and stuck it on.

"Ketchup?" Finley frowned. "What food group is that?"

"Duh, vegetable," said Evie. "It's made from tomatoes."

"A tomato is a fruit," said Finley.

Henry crinkled his brow. "Wait, so ketchup is a *fruit?*"

Finley sighed and handed him the labels. "Your turn."

"Sorry," said Henry. "I need to ketchup. Get it — *catch up?*"

"Bwah-ha-ha." Evie let out a loud fake laugh. "We get it."

"Hmmm . . ." said Henry. "I'm going to go with whipped cream. That would be dairy. Or I could do Swiss cheese. Or maybe —"

· "Whipped cream," Finley said, passing him the pencil. Sometimes it Henry took *forever* to make a decision.

"Right," said Henry. "Whipped cream makes everything better." He wrote it down and handed the pencil back to Finley.

Finley thought for a minute then wrote *cauliflower* in the next space.

"*Cauliflower?*" Henry wrinkled his nose. "That's completely random."

Finley shrugged. "I love cauliflower. It's an under-appreciated vegetable."

Evie took the pencil. "How do you spell *capers?*" she asked.

"Capers?" Henry asked, raising an eyebrow.

Evie ran to the kitchen and came back carrying a jar of little green balls. "Capers." She handed the jar to Henry. "They're pickled flower buds. Dad puts them on his sandwiches."

"Really?" Finley grabbed the jar and studied the little bobbing balls. She dug around and fished one out, then held it up for closer inspection.

They sure don't look like flower buds, she thought. *They look like boogers.*

"They're yummy," said Evie. "Try one."

Henry made a face. "No, thanks. I'm good."

Finley was known for being a brave eater, and she wasn't about to let some booger-ball flower bud ruin her reputation. She scowled at it, then popped it into her mouth and made a fish face. "Ack! Pthffft! Salty!"

"Yep," Evie said with a grin. "That's why I like them."

Finley, Henry, and Evie took turns writing different ingredients until all the pie-shaped spaces on the spinner were full. They also added a chocolate food group. (Because as Evie pointed out: everyone needs chocolate.) Then Finley passed the spinner to Evie.

"All right," said Henry. "Give it a whirl, girl. Spin to win!"

Evie spun the arrow. "Yay!" she said, clapping her hands. "It stopped on chocolate syrup! What are the chances of that?"

"One in twelve," said Henry, pointing at the spinner spaces. He spun next. "Yes! Whipped cream."

Finley's arrow landed on orange juice.

"So far, so good," said Evie. "This is fun! How many times do we go?"

Finley looked at Henry. "So far we've got a dairy, a fruit, and a chocolate — that's three of our six food groups. Should we keep spinning until the recipe looks done?"

"How about till we get one thing from each food group?" said Henry. "Then it'll be a balanced meal. Plus, every spin is another chance it'll land on capers. Let's quit while we're ahead."

"Okay," said Evie. She crossed her fingers and spun the arrow. They watched as it slowed and came to rest. "Smoked salmon," she said. "There's our protein."

"Hoo-boy," said Henry, shaking his head. "I'm not liking the sound of this." He spun and got applesauce, but they already had a fruit, so he tried again and got oatmeal.

Finley took a turn. "Corn," she said. "That's a veggie, and oatmeal's a grain, so we're done."

Finley put the ingredients into a bowl, and they all took turns mashing and mixing them together into a brownish-pinkish, gluey-looking glop.

"Ooh," said Evie. "That looks a little funky."

"It *smells* a little funky." Finley held out the spoon. "Want a lick?"

Evie backed away. "Uh-uh. You can have it."

Finley put the spoon in the sink.

"What *is* it?" said Henry.

"It's a drink," said Finley. "A smoked salmon smoothie." She poured the lumpy liquid into a glass. *Glunk, glunk, glunk.*

"Whoa," said Henry. "That's what you get when you cook by chance. Do you think we should start over?"

"No way," said Finley. "That's cheating."

Finley and Evie got out more glasses and set the table.

When Mom came home a few minutes later, Finley met her at the door and took her coat. "Welcome home, Mom. Your dinner's waiting."

"How lovely," said Mom, her eyes darting around the kitchen. "What's that smell?"

Finley wiggled her eyebrows. "It's a surprise." Finley led Mom to the dining room table and pulled out her chair. They usually ate in the kitchen, but this dinner was special. "Have a seat and relax," she said. "I'll be right back."

Finley filled the rest of the glasses, making sure they were even. Then she squirted a blob of whipped cream on top of each one. "There," she said. "Much better. Evie, tell Dad and Zack dinner's ready."

"Daaaaaad! Zaaaaack! Dinner's ready!" Evie yelled.

When everyone came to the table, Finley, Henry, and Evie carried in the drinks.

"Wow," said Mom. "You made dinner all by yourselves?" She gave Dad a look. Dad just shrugged and smiled.

"What *is* it?" Zack asked.

Finley set a drink down in front of him, then passed Mom and Dad theirs. "It's 'Dinner in a Glass,'" she said proudly. "A Smoked Salmon Smoothie — nutritious and convenient, a balanced meal on-the-go."

Suddenly, Zack pushed his chair back and stood up. "Speaking of, I gotta go."

"Where?" Dad asked.

"I have to do . . . homework! *Tons* of homework! And I've got a major test tomorrow. If I don't start studying, I'll fail for sure." Zack mouthed "good luck" and went to grab his books.

Mom cupped her hand to her ear. "Is that my cell phone ringing? I'm expecting a call." She headed for the kitchen. "I'll be back. Go ahead and start without me."

Dad looked at his drink, then at Henry.

Henry looked at Evie.

Evie looked at Finley.

"All right," said Finley, raising her glass. "Down the hatch!"

She brought the glass to her lips. It smelled like a blend of chocolate, cat food, and air freshener. She pinched her nose and waited for someone else to take a sip. "What are you all waiting for?" she asked.

"What are *you* waiting for?" asked Henry.

"Drink on the count of three," said Finley. "One . . . two . . . three!"

Finley took a big gulp and looked up just in time to see Henry gagging. As the flavor hit her taste buds, her eyes started to water. It was definitely not Fin-tastic. It was *awful*. Trying not to spew, she sprinted to the kitchen sink. She spit out the smoothie and rinsed her mouth under the faucet until her tongue was numb.

When she turned around, Henry was stumbling toward her with a help-I'm-gonna-hurl face, and Evie was frantically rummaging through the basket-of-found-things on the kitchen counter.

"Here!" said Evie, digging out some restaurant mints and throwing one to Henry. "I'm gonna go brush my teeth for about five days!"

Henry ripped the wrapper open and popped the mint into his mouth. Then he slumped on a kitchen chair and glowered at Finley.

"Are you okay?" Finley asked. "You don't look so good."

"I don't *feel* so good," he croaked. "That tasted like garbage. You know, that wasn't fair — you didn't even swallow yours."

"How could I?" said Finley. "I saw the look on your face. So much for 'Dinner in a Glass.' I guess nutritious and delicious don't always go together."

"Ugh." Henry shuddered and put his head down on the table. "I've changed my mind. Whipped cream does *not* make everything better."

"Look, I'll make it up to you," said Finley. "We'll be laughing about this when we're eating *free pizza for a whole year.*"

Henry groaned. "If I ever eat again."

When Finley went back to the dining room, Dad had the phone in his hand.

"What are you doing?" she said.

Dad gave her an I'm-sorry look. "Ordering take-out."

* * *

After Henry left, Finley tried to think of a new plan. The cook-off was in two days, and they weren't any closer to a winning recipe than when they'd started. She was sitting at the kitchen table when Zack came in and started rooting around in the fridge.

"Have you seen the chocolate syrup?" he asked.

"It's gone," said Finley. "We used it for the smoothies."

Zack shook his head. "This cooking contest thing is out of control. There's nothing left in the fridge except your crazy concoctions."

Finley sighed. "You can make fun all you want. Wait till we win. If you're lucky we'll give you a slice of our Flying Pie pizza."

Zack smirked. "That's the only thing you could give me that I'd actually eat."

"Too bad," said Finley. "You don't know what you're missing."

Zack got a pen and took the shopping list off the fridge. "I know exactly what I'm missing. Chocolate syrup."

Finley wouldn't let Zack crush her creative spirit. He was probably still mad about last Christmas when she'd craft-ified his baseball card collection and made it into a seriously snappy scrapbook. (Turned out he wasn't a big fan of glitter glue and stick-on jewels.)

Finley took a bath and went to bed early. She tried lying on her back, her front, and her side. She even tried lying with her head where her feet should be, but she couldn't get to sleep. She kept thinking about all of their botched recipes. Pretty much everything they'd made had famously flopped. They'd even managed to wreck all their favorite foods. Their chances of winning the cook-off were looking slim.

But Finley knew she couldn't let Henry down. She pictured him blowing out birthday candles on the cheesiest, most perfectly crusted, deeply topped, extra-extra-largest Flying Pie pizza ever.

Surely they could come up with *something* that tasted good.

But could they do it in time?

Chapter 7
KA-POW!

The next morning, Finley felt like she hadn't slept at all. Her dreams had been full of monster marshmallows, vampire pickles, and zombie meatloaf. When her alarm went off, she'd been sinking in a bottomless pit of honey mustard.

Henry came over right after soccer. They had one day to come up with a winning recipe, and Finley's head was as empty as the fridge.

"Come on, Fin," Henry said. "Use your imagination."

Finley sighed heavily. "My imagination is on vacation."

"Bad timing."

Finley nodded. "No joke." She tapped her pencil on the table. "Well, we've learned that nutritious does not equal delicious."

"Exactly," said Henry.

"And that lot of food combinations are just plain wrong," Finley continued.

Henry nodded. "Really, *really* wrong."

"So maybe we need to start with something we know is really *right*," said Finley. "We could put a new twist on an old standard. Something that's stood the test of time."

"How?" Henry asked.

"Fusion food," Finley whispered, her eyes wide.

Henry raised an eyebrow. "Sounds dangerous."

Finley shook her head. "No, it's perfectly safe. Mom told me about it. She and Dad had it at a fancy restaurant. You just combine two different dishes in an interesting way. Like, say, sushi nachos."

"Ew." Henry made a face.

"Okay, bad example. But you get the idea. All we have to do is find two popular dishes that go great together but that nobody *knows* go great together."

"All right," said Henry. "What foods can we fuse?"

"The possibilities are in-Fin-ite," said Finley. "First we need some fun foods. What about hot dogs? They pretty much scream fun. That's why they serve them at baseball games and the county fair. Or popcorn. Or Popsicles. Hey, what about hot-dog Popsicles?"

"You mean *cold* dogs?" Henry frowned. "Not so fun."

"Chocolate mac and cheese?" Finley suggested.

"Uh-uh," said Henry. "Don't mess with the mac."

Finley opened the fridge and drew in her breath. "Score! Leftover spaghetti noodles!"

"That could work," said Henry. "Pasta is totally timeless. It's been around since ancient China."

Finley looked at Henry. "How do you know this stuff?"

"The cooking channel."

Finley pictured people eating pasta through the ages. For thousands of years, humans had lived and played and worked and grown old — all while eating pasta. Suddenly, cooking with pasta seemed like an awesome responsibility. They'd have to combine it with something equally inspiring. But what?

Just then Zack came in and started searching through the cupboards.

Finley glared at her brother. He was always hungry. He must be going through another growth spurt or something. That's what Mom always said.

"You guys just don't quit, do you?" Zack said. He took out a jar of peanut butter and some grape jelly and smeared them on some bread. "The cook-off is tomorrow, right? You should stick to something simple. Like good ol' PB&J."

Finley frowned. "We don't need your help, Zack."

"Suit yourself." Zack grabbed his sandwich and retreated to his lair.

Finley started to put away the peanut butter. "Wait!" she said. "What about peanut butter and jelly? Everyone likes PB&J. Just like everyone likes pasta. Peanut-butter-and-jelly pasta — it's practically the perfect fusion food!" Finley got out another jar of peanut butter. "What do you think," she said, "smooth or crunchy?"

"Crunchy?" Henry looked nervous.

"Good call." Finley spooned out globs of peanut butter and dropped them into the leftover pasta. "Never underestimate the importance of texture. Now for the jelly. Grape or strawberry?"

"Definitely grape," said Henry.

Finley handed him the jar. Henry spooned it in and tossed the noodles until they were coated with brown and purple blobs. "Yikes," he said. "It sure *looks* original."

"Let's find out," said Finley. She wound a couple of noodles around the end of a fork and took a bite. It tasted like a slippery, stringy, peanut-butter-and-jelly sandwich.

"Hmm," Finley said, chewing. "It still needs something." She snapped her fingers. "I know —

how about a little spice?" She opened the fridge and picked out a tiny bottle. "Hot sauce. This'll give it some pizzazz." She took off the cap and shook the bottle over the pasta.

"KA-POW!" said Henry. "There's the flavor explosion. But isn't that kind of a lot?"

"It could use a little bit of kick," said Finley, mixing it in. "It'll be KA-POWerful." She passed him a forkful.

"Why me?" Henry asked, backing away.

"Because I already tried it," said Finley. "And because you're the picky one. If *you* like it, anybody will."

"Good point." Henry eyed the gooey noodles, then took a mouthful.

"So?" said Finley, watching him chew.

Henry's eyes bulged. His cheeks got red. "Water!" he whispered, fanning his face.

Finley handed him a glassful, which he chugged in two seconds flat.

"It's KA-POWerful, all right," he squeaked. "That's not fusion food — it's *con-fusion* food." Henry took off his hat and shoved it into his backpack.

"What are you doing?" Finley asked.

"I'm *Fin*-ished," Henry croaked.

"You can't give up." Finley pouted. "We're just getting started!"

"Easy for you to say," said Henry. "You're not the one whose taste buds got burned off."

"Fine," said Finley. "Be a quitter. But we'll never win if we don't even try."

Henry's face got three shades redder. "We've been trying for days, and everything we've come up with has been nasty. You never listen to me. Everything always has to be *your* way. I'm sick of being the guinea pig in your cooking experiments. You're on your own!"

With that, Henry slung his backpack over his shoulder and walked out.

Finley's stomach sank. She went to the window and watched Henry pedal away. She and Henry didn't fight. When they saw things differently, they always agreed to disagree. But she'd never seen him this mad.

Maybe he'll come around, she told herself. *Maybe I can still win the contest and give him the free pizza for his birthday. Then he'll be happy.*

Finley inspected the pasta, dangling a limp piece of spaghetti from her fork. Plenty of people liked spicy. And Henry was kind of a wimp when it came to food. Besides, they'd used all the noodles. It was going to have to do.

Finley gave the dish a final stir and shoved some paper drink umbrellas into it for decoration.

"There," she said. "PB&J Pasta. I just hope we made enough."

Chapter 8
BUGS ON A LOG

The next day was cook-off day. Finley woke up early, made a sign for her table, and gathered her supplies. She checked to see if Henry had called, but he hadn't. After lunch, Finley packed up her pasta, and Dad gave her a ride to school. Now that all the cooking was done, she could relax and have fun. If only her stomach would stop flip-flopping.

By the time she got there, the gym was bustling. Contestants were busy setting up food on long tables.

Families strolled the aisles, sneaking peeks at the dishes. There were cookies, cakes, and tofu dogs in a blanket. There was s'mores casserole and plenty of potato salad. But there was no sign of Henry.

Dad and Evie walked Finley in and offered to help set up, but she wanted to do it on her own.

"Good luck, and have fun, Chef Flowers," Dad said, kissing her head. "We'll be back in a bit."

Finley followed the crowd toward a hovering bundle of purple balloons. When she got closer, she heard classical music and saw a tent draped with purple streamers. A banner with the words "Lavender Lemonade" in swirly letters hung across the front.

Olivia Snotham was sitting under it in a frilly purple dress. She looked like a purple princess.

"Would you care to sample some lemonade?" Olivia asked in her syrupy-sweet way.

Finley stole a glance at the fancy drink dispenser filled with lavender liquid and floating lemon slices. She was pretty thirsty. And it looked pretty good. But there was no way she was going to try it. She didn't want to give Olivia the satisfaction.

"No, thanks," said Finley, walking on by. Then she spotted her name card on the next row of tables and went to claim her place.

She put out a jar to collect food tickets and arranged sample cups and napkins on the plastic tablecloth Mom had dug out of the party drawer. Then she propped up her sign, which had the words "PB&J PASTA" printed in grape-jelly-colored glitter glue on peanut-

butter-colored paper, with dried pasta stuck all around it. It looked pretty small next to Olivia's display, but she hadn't had much time to make it.

No worries, Finley told herself. *It's the food that matters. All I have to do is get one person to try it and then wait for the word to spread.*

As families started trickling down the aisles, Finley scanned the room, looking for Henry. She didn't think he'd show up, but she wished he would. After all, his birthday was the reason she was there in the first place.

Soon most of the tables were taken. Finley felt like a tiny island in a sea of people. Suddenly she spotted Henry talking to Mr. Spark, and her heart leaped. Henry caught her eye and gave a little wave.

Yay! Finley thought. *He came to say he's sorry and rejoin the team!*

Henry looked like he was on his way over, but at the last minute, he turned and headed for one of the empty tables in the corner, pulling a small rolling suitcase behind him.

Finley watched as he unpacked it and sat down. *Unbelievable*, she thought. *He's not on my team. He's my competition.* She craned her neck to get a glimpse of what he'd made, but all she could see was a bunch of plastic containers and a stack of plates and napkins. Then a bunch of kids blocked her view. Whatever his dish was, it couldn't be very original. He'd probably copied something from one of his dumb shows.

Finley arranged and rearranged her forks and practiced her talk on fusion food, but people kept passing her by. She figured they were just checking out all the offerings before they bought. She smiled to herself. *They'll be back.*

Finley took out a pen and started doodling on a napkin. She doodled until she ran out of space. When she looked up, Olivia's table had a long line. Her awful music and purple poof princess dress seemed to be working. It was royally annoying.

Finley wished she could talk to Henry. He always made her feel better. She grabbed another napkin and started sketching him in his chef's hat and apron. She made sure to include his dimples and to curve his right eyebrow up just so.

"Hi," a voice said.

Finley looked up to see Henry standing there with his hands shoved in his pockets.

"How's business?" he asked, glancing at her drawing.

"Okay." Finley flipped the napkin over fast. "You?"

Henry looked at his shoes. "Same."

Finley twirled her hair. "So what did you make?"

"I started with Fire Ants on a Log."

"What's that?"

"It's like regular Ants on a Log. You know, raisins lined up on a celery stick filled with cream cheese? But I used cranberries instead. That's what makes them fire ants. I figured I should stick to something I like, so I came up with a whole Bugs on a Log series. Ticks on a Log — those are chocolate chips. Termites on a Log with peanuts. Cockroaches on a Log with figs. Larvae on a Log with mini-marshmallows — those were the best. And Lice on a Log with sprinkled sesame seeds."

"Oh." Finley met Henry's eyes. They stayed that way for a minute before Henry's cheeks got pink, and he looked away. "Good idea."

"Thanks. The little kids seemed to like them." Henry looked at his watch and glanced around the room. "Well, I'd better get back."

"Hey," Finley said as he turned to go. "Maybe we could share a table. Then at least we could talk. I mean, if you don't mind . . ."

"Sure," said Henry. "I'm done anyway. I was just going to clean up." He went to collect his things.

Finley felt sorry for him. He must not have sold very many samples if he was already finished. And who could blame people for passing up something so gross? Ants on a Log was a classic snack. But Lice on a Log? Yuck. It made her head itch just thinking about it.

Chapter 9
THIRST FOR FIRST

By the time Henry got back, the line for Olivia's lemonade wrapped halfway around the gym.

"I just don't get it," said Finley. "Lavender is a smell, not a flavor. I bet that lemonade tastes like soap."

"It *is* original. And it looks pretty thirst-quenching." Henry fished around in his pockets and pulled out two tickets. "In fact, I could go for a glass right about now. Want one?"

Finley grabbed his arm. "Don't even think about it." She glared in Olivia's direction. "Gol-*ly*, that music is loud. We've got to let people know we're over here, too." She climbed onto her chair and cupped her hands around her mouth. "Get your PB&J Pasta!" she yelled above the noise. "Try something truly tasty today!"

Olivia must have heard that, because she looked right at Finley and scowled, then turned up the volume and went back to fake smiling.

"Step right up!" Finley shouted over Olivia's blaring symphony. "You'll be happy you did!"

A couple of lemonade drinkers wandered over to have a look.

"Here you go," said Mr. Spark. He held out a food ticket.

"Congratulations!" Finley jumped down from the chair and handed her teacher a sample cup. "You're our first customer!"

"Well, aren't I lucky?" said Mr. Spark. He winked at Finley and Henry. Then he took a big mouthful of noodles.

"Ka-pow," whispered Henry as he watched Mr. Spark chew.

"So," Finley said, "what do you think?"

Suddenly, Mr. Spark's face went as red as a tomato. His smile froze. His mustache quivered. His eyes got glassy. He looked like he'd swallowed a live rattlesnake. "Mm-*hmm*," he said, nodding slowly. Then he gave them an a-okay sign and disappeared into the crowd.

"I don't think it was his cup of tea," said Henry in his best British accent. "But at least you sold one."

"At least *we* sold one," Finley corrected.

Finley and Henry watched the lemonade line get longer. They played hangman and tic-tac-toe and charades. They stacked their extra sample cups into pyramids and took turns knocking them down.

Finley was rummaging around in her bag trying to find more napkins when Zack ambled up to her table.

"All right, little sis," he said, handing her a ticket. "One bowl of Pasta Disasta."

"For your information, it's PB&J Pasta," said Finley.

"What does PB&J stand for?" Zack asked. "Pretty Bad Joke?"

"Ha, ha, ha. You're *so* funny," said Finley. "It's probably too good for you anyway."

"Come on." Zack grinned. "I can take it."

Finley handed Zack a sample and watched him scoop up a giant forkful. As he chewed, his grin disappeared, and he got that serious look like when he was up to bat with two strikes and the bases loaded. His forehead started to sweat. He put a hand up to his mouth.

"So?" Finley said. "What do you think?"

But Zack was already speed-walking to the water fountain.

"Look at that," said Finley. "It was so good, he was speechless."

Their next customer was Maggie Martin, across-the-street-Kate's older sister. She was in Zack's class at Woodland Middle School and was known for beating all the boys at dodgeball. She also held the school record for most sit-ups in a minute. She looked at Finley and plunked down a ticket. "Let's see what all the fuss is about."

"Just the most original dish ever," Finley said, passing her some pasta.

Maggie ate the whole sample in one heaping bite. Then she looked at Finley like she'd just been socked in the stomach. "WHOOOO-EEEE!" she hollered, making a beeline for the bathroom. "HO-O-O-T STUUUUUFF!"

Everyone — even Olivia — turned to watch her streak by.

Finley had a handful more customers. Her friends Lia and Kate traded one of their chocolate-mint brownies for some pasta. Mom and Dad came by and took a bunch of pictures, sampled a bite, and left in a hurry. Mom mumbled something about needing to talk to one of the other parents, and Dad gave a thumbs-up, we're-so-proud-of-you sign and followed her, fanning himself. Principal Small even tried some. (Her face turned the color of her lipstick.)

Soon, a line had formed at Finley's table. The line got longer. Word was spreading! Henry collected the tickets, and Finley served up samples. It was hard to tell if people liked it. Once they'd taken a bite, they didn't say much. Finley figured they were just blown away by the Fin-omenal flavor.

After a while, the line got shorter. Once the last person had been served, Finley tidied up the table. She put her hand in the jar and swirled the tickets around. It was only half full, but it was a pretty big jar. She gave Henry a fist bump and sat back in her chair.

"So what do *you* think of PB&J Pasta?" said Henry.

Finley shrugged. "I don't know. I haven't tried it since I added the KA-POW."

"*What?*" Henry's eyebrows shot up. "How can you sell it when you haven't even tasted it?"

"I don't have to taste it to know it's original," Finley told him.

"Here," Henry said, holding out a cup and a fork. "You *have* to taste it."

Finley took the cup. "Fine." She twirled one strand of spaghetti around the fork and took a nibble. At first the flavor was all peanut butter and grape. Then came the heat. It smoldered and sparked and burst into a fire that filled her mouth and spread through her whole body.

Her fingers flamed.

Her toes tingled.

"Here, drink!" said Henry, handing her a water bottle.

Finley guzzled it down. "Thanks," she said, panting. "Phew! That packs a punch!"

Looking up, Finley noticed that all of the people who had just eaten her pasta were back in line for lavender lemonade. "Hey!" she said. "No fair — they're getting seconds."

"Yep," Henry said, nodding. "And I'm pretty sure I know why."

Chapter 10
SWEET SUCCESS

At three o'clock sharp, Principal Small had the parent volunteers collect all the ticket jars from the participants' tables and announced that everyone should gather in the auditorium in half an hour.

"Wow. Looks like you sold a lot," Finley said as Henry handed in his jar.

Henry shrugged. "I guess bugs are popular with kindergarteners," he said. "Carter's little brother tried them all."

"Well, that does it," said Finley. "I don't have a chance — I didn't get as many tickets as you."

Henry picked up the contest information sheet. "It says here that the judges will give points for ticket sales *and* for originality. You've still got a great chance. Yours was definitely the most original."

"You really think so?" Finley said hopefully.

Henry nodded. "No joke."

Finley and Henry packed up their stuff and headed for the auditorium. They slipped through the doors and stood at the back.

At three-thirty, Principal Small clip-clopped onto the stage and took the microphone. Finley noticed her cheeks still had a healthy PB&J Pasta glow.

"Good afternoon, everyone," said Principal Small. "Thanks so much for coming to the first annual Glendale Elementary School Cook-Off. I sampled so many fantastic dishes today, I think we should make a Glendale cookbook. Before I announce the winning recipe, remember that everyone's a winner, as the money raised from this event will go toward building a new playground we can all enjoy."

Right, thought Finley. *But there's only one first-place ribbon and year's worth of free pizza.*

Just then Olivia appeared with two cups of lemonade. "Here," she said, holding them out to Finley and Henry. "The last ones. My treat."

"Thanks," said Henry. He gulped his down and wiped his mouth with his hand. "That's really good."

"No thanks," said Finley, even though her mouth was still burning and lemonade sounded like just the thing to put out the fire.

"Suit yourself," said Olivia. "Cheers."

As Finley watched Olivia sip her drink, she could feel the heat spread to her cheeks. Why did Olivia have to be so prim, so proper, so . . . *perfect*?

Principal Small cleared her throat. "I know you're all anxious to hear who will get a year's worth of Flying Pie pizza. So let's get to it. Today's winner, based on overall tickets sold, and a truly original recipe . . ."

Oh, come on, already, thought Finley. Her heart thumped. Her stomach squeezed. PB&J Pasta was truly original. It was a little on the spicy side, but so what? Could it be? Could they possibly win? She couldn't wait a second longer. She had to know.

"Is . . ." Principal Small looked in her direction.

Finley felt faint. It was all she could do not to run right up to the podium and break into her happy dance. She'd practiced her acceptance speech and had a list of people to thank just in case. She couldn't wait to see Henry's face when they won. He'd be the first one she'd thank. Then she'd give him the prize and wish him happy birthday in front of all those people.

"Olivia Snotham and her lavender lemonade!" Principal Small finished with a smile.

As the tidal wave of disappointment hit her, there was a high-pitched squeal in Finley's ear. Olivia squeezed out from beside her and wove her way through the crowd to the stage, where she curtsied and blew kisses. She held up her glass of lemonade and said something about success being sweet. Then she took a drink and curtsied some more. The crowd clapped and cheered.

Finley tried to push the ugly thoughts out of her head. She tried to be happy for Olivia. But she couldn't help being jealous. Once again, Olivia was a winner. And that made Finley and Henry losers.

Olivia was still bowing and saying thank you when Principal Small handed her a humongous first-place ribbon. Olivia held it up and beamed.

Finley couldn't stand to keep watching. She snuck out through the auditorium doors and slunk down the hall to the gym.

As Finley picked up her things, she heard a round of applause. She wished Dad would hurry up. Soon the gym would be swarming with people, and she didn't feel like talking to anyone. Especially Olivia.

But when she turned to go, Olivia was standing right there wearing her sugarcoated grin. "Your pasta looked really . . . interesting," she said. "Good idea, making the weirdest recipe ever so people would be curious and buy a sample. And your brother was funny, daring everyone to try it."

Before Finley could think of anything to say, Olivia had walked away.

A *dare?* Finley thought. That was the real reason she'd sold some? There she was thinking people actually liked it, when Zack had been making a game out of it?

Finley felt sick. *I will not cry*, she told herself. *I will absolutely not cry.*

Finley was about to bolt for the door when she felt a hand on her shoulder.

"Hey, are you okay?" It was Henry.

Finley blinked back the tears. "I'm great," she said. "Just great."

"Come on," said Henry. "It's not so bad."

Finley frowned. "It's not so good."

"It's good for Olivia," Henry said. "And good for the school. She sold a ton of lemonade to raise money for the playground."

"Yeah," said Finley glumly. "She couldn't have done it without me. My spicy pasta sure spiced up her sales. People were dying for a drink."

"We didn't win, but it was fun trying," said Henry. "Well . . . most of the time."

"It would have been *more* fun to win," said Finley.

"But guess what?" said Henry, his eyes lighting up. "You missed the best part! After you left, Principal Small announced they weren't planning on having a runner-up, but the judges were so impressed with my entry, they wanted to give me a certificate of achievement." Henry's cheeks turned pink as he held it up. "I got to meet Chef George from The Flying Pie. He said I could drop by sometime to help out."

Finley read the certificate. "Wow," she said. "That's great! Congratulations."

"Thanks." Henry tucked it into his notebook. "Hey, you look like you could use a joke."

"Sure," said Finley.

"Why did the eggs die laughing?"

"I don't know," Finley said.

Henry raised his eyebrows. "Because they cracked each other up."

Finley couldn't help but smile.

Just then Olivia walked by with her big blue ribbon. "See you on Monday," she said.

"Congratulations," Henry said. "Bang-up job on that lemonade."

"Yeah," muttered Finley. "Congratulations."

"Thanks," said Olivia. "I can't wait for my pizza."

As Finley watched her walk away, she wondered if Olivia had anyone to share it with. Suddenly, Finley wasn't so mad anymore. In fact, she felt a little sorry for her.

* * *

Henry got a ride home with Finley and wound up staying for dinner. The whole way home, Evie couldn't stop talking about Olivia's "groovy" purple lemonade.

Finley couldn't stop thinking about Olivia enjoying her victory pizza at The Flying Pie. Mom and Dad offered to pick one up, but she wasn't in the mood.

"I know," said Mom. "We could have your leftover PB&J Pasta."

"Yeah," said Dad. "It was really . . . something."

Finley glanced at Henry. He looked like someone had just stomped on his toe. "No thanks," she said. "What about plain old peanut-butter-and-jelly sandwiches? We'll make them ourselves."

"Yes!" said Evie.

Henry smiled. "Perfect."

When they got home, Evie went to watch TV while Finley and Henry carried in the cook-off supplies and got out the sandwich stuff.

"Grape?" Finley held up the jelly jar.

"Definitely." Henry poured milk into two tall glasses. "Hey, I'm really sorry I didn't stick with you."

"*I'm* sorry I burned your mouth off," said Finley, spreading peanut butter on some bread. "I should have listened to you. I guess my Flower Power doesn't work with food. If it weren't for me, you would have come in first place. Everyone bought more of Olivia's lemonade after getting KA-POWed by my peppery pasta."

"If it weren't for you, I wouldn't have even tried," Henry said. "And I wouldn't have discovered how much I love cooking and gotten to meet Chef George and everything."

"Glad I did *something* right." Finley passed Henry his plate. "I have to admit, those Bugs on a Log were a really good idea."

"Thanks." Henry raised his glass. "To good ideas and good ol' PB&J!"

Finley grinned. Henry was a Fin-tastic friend. But as they clinked their glasses together, her stomach sank. Tomorrow was Monday — Henry's last single-digit birthday — and she still didn't have a gift.

Chapter 11
OH, BROTHER

After Henry left for the night, Finley flopped down on her bed. She was tired. So tired she could barely move. "Oooofff," she said softly.

As she watched the darkening sky out her window there was a tapping on the door. It opened a crack, and Zack peeked through.

"What are you up to?" he asked.

Finley lifted her head, then let it fall back on her pillow. "Not much. Just wondering why my own brother dared people to try my cooking."

Zack opened the door a little wider. "Mind if I come in?"

"That's never stopped you before," Finley told him.

"Look, I'm sorry," he said. "I was just trying to help. At least you sold *some*, right?"

Finley sat up. "It's so embarrassing. I'd rather not have sold any at all."

Zack cleared a spot and sat on the bed. "Did you see the look on Principal Small's face when she tasted it? Priceless."

The corners of Finley's mouth crept up before she could stop them.

"Of all those dishes, yours was *definitely* the most original," Zack said.

"More like the most ridiculous," said Finley. "I should never have tried to cook. From now on, I'll stick to crafty stuff."

Zack picked up a scrapbook from Finley's bedside table and leafed through it. "Remember the time my baseball team got eliminated in the first round of the junior tournament?"

"No." As far as Finley could remember, Zack's team always won.

"Well, we did. The Pikeville Possums totally creamed us — the little punks. And it only made it worse that everyone was sure we'd win."

"Yeah." Finley nodded. "I know what you mean. It's the hope that gets you." She wrapped herself up in her blanket.

"Wanna play cards?" said Zack. "I could use the practice."

"No, thanks," said Finley. "I just need to mope. Besides, I've already lost enough for one day."

"Well, mope away," Zack said. "But when you're done, maybe you could make me a snack?"

"Maybe." Finley smiled. "If you're brave enough to eat it. Thanks for coming to the cook-off."

"No worries. Dad bribed me with game tickets." Zack started to close the door behind him, then poked his head back in. "Just so you know, that lavender lemonade? Tasted like soap."

* * *

After Zack left, Finley lay back and stared at the ceiling. For a minute, she could almost feel the earth turning and gravity pulling her up against it, holding her in place. She imagined she was flying. She was a bird — a hawk maybe, or a big black crow. She could see her house, and her neighbor Mrs. Elliot in her garden next door. Then she swooped down the street to Henry's. Flying higher, Finley could see the whole city. Suddenly, the cook-off and Olivia and Henry seemed so small.

Then it hit her — she still didn't have a present for Henry's birthday! He'd probably made some kind of birthday wish list in his notebook. If only she'd peeked at it and gotten something he really wanted instead of wasting time trying to win that stupid contest. Now she was stuck with nothing. Unless . . .

Finley pulled her craft box out from under the bed.

Chapter 12
BIRTHDAY BOY

The next day, Finley could hardly wait to walk home from school. She'd thought about giving Henry his present at lunch or recess, but there'd been too many people around. Finley and Henry always walked together on days when he didn't have to go to soccer or the after-school program. It was only a couple of blocks to their street, but walking home made Finley feel big.

When they came to Henry's favorite tree — a cherry with blossom-covered branches — she stopped and pulled his present out from her backpack. "Happy birthday!" she said, handing it to him.

"Wow," said Henry, opening the sparkly, sticker-covered card.

HAPPY BIRTHDAY!!!
From Finley
10 GREAT THINGS ABOUT HENRY:

1) He knows all sorts of amazing facts, like that Green Bay, Wisconsin, is the toilet paper capital of the world.
2) The crinkle he gets in his forehead when he's thinking.
3) His perfect printing.
4) Ben Franklin is his favorite founding father because he invented the lightning rod and America's first library.
5) He's super ticklish, and when he laughs really hard, he makes a noise like a seal.
6) He knows his stinkbugs from his beetles.
7) He is very . . . v-e-r-y . . . v-e-rrrrr-y . . . p . . . a . . . t . . . i . . . e . . . . n . . . . t.
8) He listens to my ideas all the way till the end. (See #7.)
9) He makes lovely Lice on a Log.
10) He has wicked soccer-playing, joke-telling, and list-making skills.
(Well, actually, that makes 12 things.)

"Aw, thanks," said Henry, his cheeks rosy. Then he unwrapped the gift. It was a book. On the cover, in big bubble letters, it read: *Henry and Finley's Hen-sational, Fin-spiring Fusion Food*. There was a photo of Henry and Finley in the middle and cutout magazine pictures of ingredients all around them.

"Cool!" said Henry, turning it over to look at the back.

"The real reason I wanted to enter the cook-off was to get you the pizza for your birthday," said Finley. "But I was so worried about winning, I didn't give your ideas a chance. I thought Principal Small's cookbook idea wasn't half bad and figured maybe we could make one of our own."

"I love it," said Henry. "But you don't believe in following recipes."

"I changed my mind," said Finley. "And our cookbook won't have recipes exactly — they'll be more like options. It's a choose-your-own cookbook. Like one of those adventure stories where you decide what happens as you read. We'll have lists of ingredients, and people can pick one thing from each list for every step of the recipe. I'll do the illustrations, and you can make the lists. *And* we'll make sure everything goes together, no matter what people pick. That way, they'll have a hundred-percent chance of creating something great."

"Hey," said Henry. "Maybe *we'll* have our own TV show one day — *Finley Flowers and Henry Lin, Creative Cooks*! We could show people how to have fun while cooking up some good grub. Our slogan could be, 'Cook Up Your Own Adventure!'"

Finley grinned. "*That's* something we're great at!" She spotted a fluffy dandelion peeking out of a sidewalk crack. She picked it, then held it out to Henry. "Here," she said. "Make a wish."

He took it and twirled it between his fingers, then blew.

Finley watched the cloud of seeds drift away. "You know, out of all the years in history, I'm glad you were born in the same one as me. What's the probability of that?"

"Next to nothing," said Henry. "I guess we're lucky."

"I guess so . . ." Finley craned her neck and looked up through crisscrossed branches to the blue sky. "Wanna come over for a birthday snack? We could start working on the cookbook."

"Sure," said Henry. "But no smoked salmon smoothies."

Finley laughed. "Deal."

Henry slid the cookbook into his backpack. "So if I'm Captain Cook, then who are you? Gourmet Girl?"

"Hmm . . ." said Finley. "What about Grub Girl?"

Henry grinned. "I like it."

A gust of wind sent down a shower of sugar-white petals. Finley and Henry stretched out their arms and ran, and for a moment it seemed they might fly.

About the Author

Jessica Young grew up in Ontario, Canada. The same things make her happy now as when she was a kid: dancing, painting, music, digging in the dirt, picnics, reading, and writing. Like Finley Flowers, Jessica loves making stuff. When she was little, she wanted to be a tap-dancing flight attendant/ veterinarian, but she's changed her mind! Jessica currently lives with her family in Nashville, Tennessee.

About the Illustrator

When Jessica Secheret was young, she had strange friends that were always with her: felt pens, colored pencils, brushes, and paint. After repainting all the walls in her house, her parents decided it was time for her to express her "talent" at an art school — the famous École Boulle in Paris. After several years at various architecture agencies, Jessica decided to give up squares, rulers, and compasses and dedicate her heart and soul to what she'd always loved — putting her own imagination on paper. Today, Jessica spends her time in her Paris studio, drawing for magazines and children's books in France and abroad.

Henry's Bugs on a Log

Be on the safe side — make sure to have an adult supervise and do the cutting!

What You'll Need:

- Celery stalks, washed and cut — make sure to have an adult do the cutting for you!
- Cream cheese
- Peanut butter (or other nut butter)
- Cranberries, chocolate chips, peanuts, figs, mini-marshmallows, sesame seeds

What To Do:

Spread cream cheese or peanut butter on the celery stalks and sprinkle on the yummy toppings of your choice. Try the following variations in Henry's "Bugs on a Log" series:

- Fire Ants on a Log – cranberries
- Ticks on a Log – chocolate chips
- Termites on a Log – peanuts
- Cockroaches on a Log – figs
- Larvae on a Log – mini-marshmallows
- Lice on a Log – sesame seeds

Finley's PB&J Pasta

Make sure you have an adult cook the pasta and add the hot sauce. It's KAPOW-erful!

What You'll Need:

- Cooked pasta, slightly warm or at room temperature — make sure to have an adult do the cooking!
- Crunchy peanut butter (or other nut butter) to taste (use creamy, if you prefer)
- Grape (or other) jelly to taste
- Dash of hot sauce (optional)

What To Do:

Toss the cooked pasta, peanut butter, and jelly in a large mixing bowl until pasta is coated with the peanut butter and jelly. If you like things spicy, get an adult to help add a dash of hot sauce to taste and mix well. Serve warm or chilled.

Ask an adult to supervise, and have fun making some Fin-tastic, Hen-sational creations!

She's always cooking up something creative – and her adventures don't end here!

Turn the page for a sneak peek at the next book in the Finley Flowers series, *Nature Calls*!

Chapter 1

READY TO ROUGH IT

Finley Flowers got her new hiking boots out of her closet and tugged them on. They were the color of rust, with thick, nubby soles, and they laced up her ankles like roller skates. They were dirt-kicking, trail-blazing, stump-stomping boots. She couldn't wait to try them out. It had only been a week since summer vacation had started, but it felt like a year. Now it was *finally* Finley's first day of overnight camp, and she was ready.

Finley tied her laces up tight and bounded down the stairs to the kitchen where her older brother, Zack, was finishing a bowl of cereal. "I'm all packed for Camp Acorn!" Finley told him. "They have so many awesome activities — fishing, archery, camp cooking, creek exploring — there's even a raft on the lake where you can make cool crafts."

"I know," Zack said, putting his bowl in the sink. "I've been going there since I was eight, remember?" He threw a box of granola bars into his backpack. "Overnight camp's not all fun and games. You have to be tough to rough it."

"I'm tough." Finley stood tall. "Tougher than you."

"Ha!" Zack smirked. "We'll see about that."

Finley frowned. "What's that supposed to mean?"

"It means I'll believe it when I see it." Zack hoisted his backpack onto his shoulder. "Everyone knows boys are tougher than girls."

"They are not!" Finley protested.

Zack gave her a sly smile. "Prove it."

As he walked away, Finley's cheeks burned. Even though he was only two years older, Zack always made her feel small. But this time he'd gone too far. She'd show him how tough girls could be.

* * *

After breakfast, Finley lugged her bag to the car. Mom offered to help, but Finley shook her head. "I'm tough enough to carry my own stuff," she said.

Zack threw his pack in the backseat and flopped in after it. He turned up his headphones and took out his *Big League Boys* baseball book. Finley's little sister, Evie, climbed in beside him with her bag of snacks and magazines.

The drive seemed to take forever. Evie whined about wanting to go to camp and sang "Ninety-Nine Bottles of Root Beer on the Wall" about a million times. Then she drank too many juice boxes, and they had to make three pit stops.

Finally, they turned down a gravel lane, bumping and scraping along the road into the woods. It was dark in the shadows of the trees, except for a few beams of sunlight that cut through the dense canopy. Overgrown bushes scratched at the car windows.

They veered right, and the woods opened up to a wide field bordered by a line of cabins. A bunch of kids were playing Frisbee on the lawn. In the distance, the lake glinted silver in the afternoon sun.

Mom parked, and Finley jumped out. She unloaded her bags and followed Mom to the camp office. Banners and T-shirts hung on the wall, and a glass case displayed mugs, bandannas, and other camp gear. Finley checked out the photo wall — it was covered with pictures of kids swimming, roasting marshmallows, hiking, and doing all kinds of camp crafts.

Finley spotted a picture of Zack from last summer. He was standing on top of a boulder, posing like he'd just climbed Mt. Everest. Finley was so excited. She had longed to go to camp for two years, and now it was her turn. She was ready to rough it!

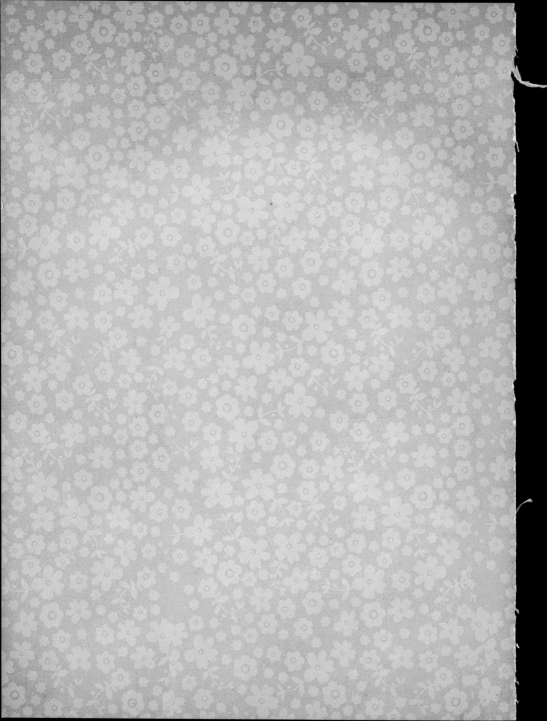